Snail Trail

Level 3A

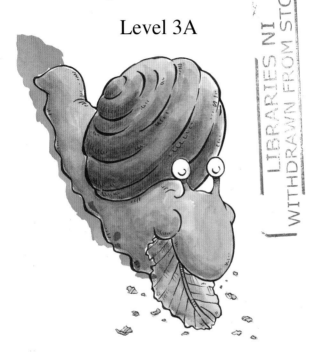

Written by Sally Grindley
Illustrated by Mike Phillips

What is synthetic phonics?

Synthetic phonics teaches children to recognise the sounds of letters and to blend 'synthesise' them together to make whole words.

Understanding sound/letter relationships gives children the confidence and ability to read unfamiliar words, without having to rely on memory or guesswork; this helps them progress towards independent reading.

Did you know? Spoken English uses more than 40 speech sounds. Each sound is called a *phoneme*. Some phonemes relate to a single letter (d-o-g) and others to combinations of letters (sh-ar-p). When a phoneme is written down it is called a *grapheme*. Teaching these sounds, matching them to their written form and sounding out words for reading is the basis of synthetic phonics.

Consultant

I love reading phonics has been created in consultation with language expert Abigail Steel. She has a background in teaching and teacher training and is a respected expert in the field of Synthetic Phonics. Abigail Steel is a regular contributor to educational publications. Her international education consultancy supports parents and teachers in the promotion of literacy skills.

Reading tips

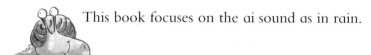

This book focuses on the ai sound as in rain.

Tricky words in this book

Any words in bold may have unusual spellings or are new and have not yet been introduced.

Tricky words in this book:

the   for   she   of   to

Extra ways to have fun with this book

After the reader has finished the story, ask them questions about what they have just read:

Why does Gail have a shock at the end of the story?
Why are the trails blue and purple?

Explain that the two letters 'ai' make one sound. Think of other words that use the 'ai' sound, such as *train* and *pain*.

I'm a fast reader. I like to read on the go!

A pronunciation guide

This grid highlights the sounds used in the story and offers a guide on how to say them.

s as in sat	a as in ant	t as in tin	p as in pig	i as in ink
n as in net	c as in cat	e as in egg	h as in hen	r as in rat
m as in mug	d as in dog	g as in get	o as in ox	u as in up
l as in log	f as in fan	b as in bag	j as in jug	v as in van
w as in wet	z as in zip	y as in yet	k as in kit	qu as in quick
x as in box	ff as in off	ll as in ball	ss as in kiss	zz as in buzz
ck as in duck	pp as in puppy	nn as in bunny	rr as in arrow	gg as in egg
dd as in daddy	bb as in chubby	tt as in attic	sh as in shop	ch as in chip
th as in them	th as in the	ng as in sing	nk as in sunk	le as in bottle
ai as in rain				

Be careful not to add an 'uh' sound to 's', 't', 'p', 'c', 'h', 'r', 'm', 'd', 'g', 'l', 'f' and 'b'. For example, say 'fff' not 'fuh' and 'sss' not 'suh'.

A snail slid from a drain
in **the** rain.

The snail slid in the paint and laid
a trail. The trail is on a pail!

The trail is on a train!

Gail, the maid, spots the trail.

'This is such a pain!' wails Gail.
'A snail has laid a trail!'

Gail gets a pail and scrubs the trail. But it is in vain!

'The snail trail has left a paint stain,' wails Gail.

Gail waits **for** the snail.

She has laid a trail **of** bait.

The snail is back!

The snail is on a raid.

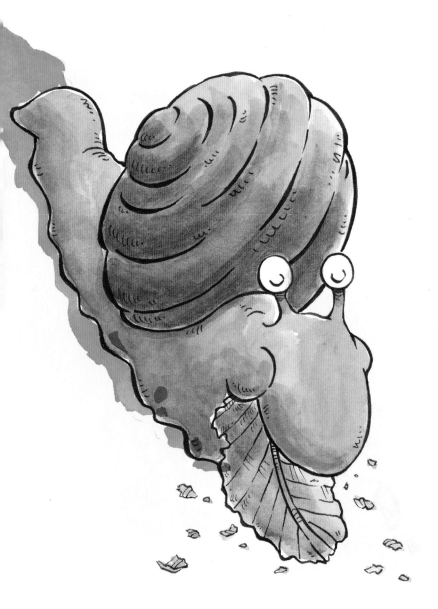

The snail slid **to** the trail of bait. Munch, munch.

Gail pops the snail in the pail.

Gail sets the snail on the grass.

Gail cannot wait to get back.

But Gail has a big shock.

A second snail has lain in wait!

OVER 48 TITLES IN SIX LEVELS
Abigail Steel recommends...

Some titles from Level 1

 **Bad Rat**
978-1-84898-277-2

 **The Best Gift**
978-1-84898-396-0

Clint and Grant Play I-Spy
978-1-84898-548-3

 Gran and Bret's Trip
978-1-84898-547-6

Some titles from Level 2

 Wish Fish
978-1-84898-386-1

 **Chuck and Duck**
978-1-84898-387-8

 Pink Bunny
978-1-84898-550-6

 Let's go to the Swings
978-1-84898-549-0

Other titles to enjoy from Level 3

 **Bart's Go-Cart**
978-1-84898-552-0

 **Queen Ella's Feet**
978-1-84898-398-4

 **Puff Flies**
978-1-84898-399-1

An Hachette UK Company
www.hachette.co.uk

Copyright © Octopus Publishing Group Ltd 2012
First published in Great Britain in 2012 by TickTock, an imprint of Octopus Publishing Group Ltd,
Endeavour House, 189 Shaftesbury Avenue, London WC2H 8JY.
www.octopusbooks.co.uk

ISBN 978 1 84898 397 7

Printed and bound in China
10 9 8 7 6 5 4 3 2